John Burningham
and Helen Oxenbury
Air Miles

Written by Bill Salaman

JONATHAN CAPE • LONDON

Miles, our much-loved difficult dog.

My husband, John, wrote two stories about Miles, our much-loved but very difficult Jack Russell – the first was titled Motor Miles. *While thinking about his second Miles story,* Air Miles, *John became very ill and realized he may not be able to finish this book. John asked me if I would finish* Air Miles *for him. At this point Miles had died, so I thought my contribution could be my homage to the two much-loved men in my life.*

Illustrating Air Miles *was not easy for many reasons. John's dear friend Bill Salaman offered to write the story as far as he remembered from what John had told him. Bill wrote a very beautiful and moving version of John's story. Three of John's illustrations are also included in the book and we have used his thumbnail sketches for the endpapers.*
HELEN OXENBURY, 2021

 *With thanks to Gordon Grant for making Miles's plane from John's sketches*

JONATHAN CAPE

UK | USA | Canada | Ireland | Australia | India | New Zealand | South Africa

Jonathan Cape is part of the Penguin Random House group of companies whose addresses can be found at global.penguinrandomhouse.com.

www.penguin.co.uk   www.puffin.co.uk   www.ladybird.co.uk

 Penguin
Random House
UK

First published 2021
001

Text copyright © The Estate of John Burningham, and William Salaman, 2021
Illustration copyright © Helen Oxenbury and John Burningham, 2021
The moral right of the authors and illustrators has been asserted

Printed in China
ISBN: 978–0–857–55219–8

The authorized representative in the EEA is Penguin Random House Ireland,
Morrison Chambers, 32 Nassau Street, Dublin D02 YH68

A CIP catalogue record for this book is available from the British Library

All correspondence to: Jonathan Cape, Penguin Random House Children's,
One Embassy Gardens, 8 Viaduct Gardens, London SW11 7BW

This is Miles.
He lives with Norman Trudge
and Norman's mother, Alice Trudge.

Miles doesn't chase
balls like he used to.

His legs hurt when
he goes for walks.

Sometimes he can't hear Norman
or Alice when they call for him.

"I think Miles needs something new
and exciting to cheer him up,"
Alice Trudge said.

"Let's ask our neighbour Mr Huddy
what he can do to help."

Mr Huddy had once made a car for Miles.

When he was younger, Miles drove it around the countryside, so Mr Huddy was the right person to ask.

"I've been making an aeroplane,"
said Mr Huddy.

"When we find a pilot who's small
enough to sit in the cockpit,
we can go to the field across
the road and try it out."

"Could Miles be your pilot?" Norman asked.
"After all, he's small and he drives a car.
Couldn't he fly your aeroplane as well?"

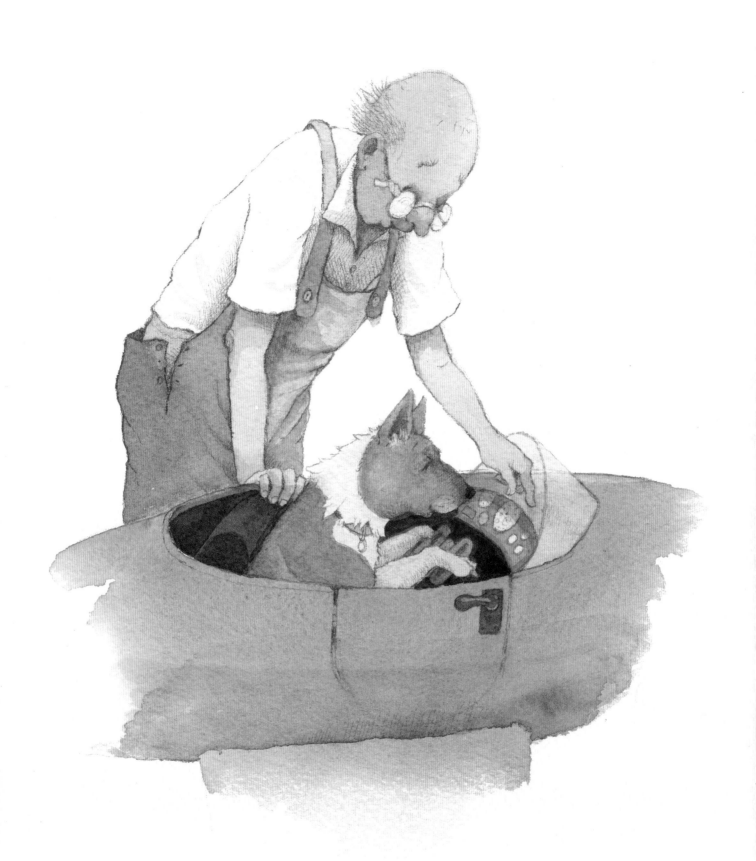

Quickly, Miles learned how to fly.

On a sunny day, with the engine roaring and the propeller whirring, the plane sped across the field and rose into the air.

Miles was flying.

Miles was tired when he returned.
Norman had to help him
out of the cockpit.

Miles slept for a whole day.

Then he flew again.
Over the lakes and the hills he went.

Along the coast.

Into the clouds.

And sometimes he flew at night . . .

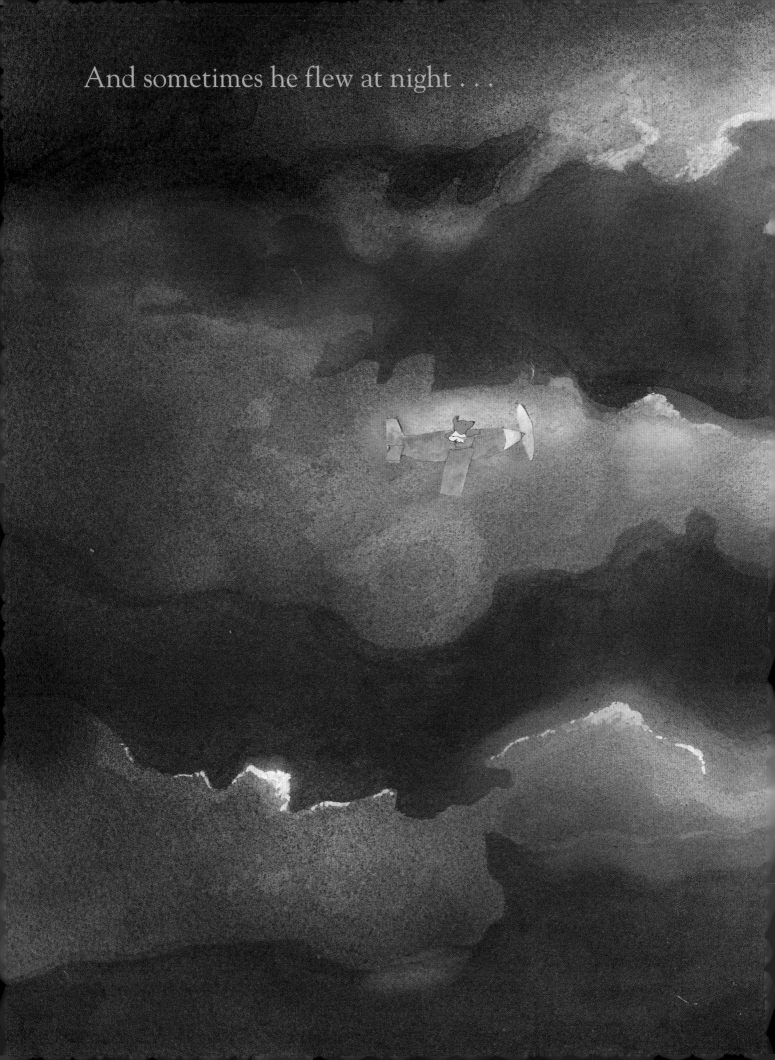

. . . exploring the country, flying across big cities.

Each time Miles landed
in the field, Norman helped
him out of the cockpit.

Soon after, Miles stopped
wanting to go for walks.
He stopped enjoying
his food.

And he even stopped flying
his plane. He seemed to
be thinking.

One day, Miles climbed out
of his basket in the kitchen
and left the house.

Norman followed him
to the field where the
plane was parked.

Gently, Norman lifted Miles into the cockpit.

The engine burst into life. Miles raced over the grass, then headed for the sky.

He flew higher than ever before.

He flew further than ever before.

Norman waved and waved
until he could see the plane
no longer.

Slowly, Norman
walked home.

Goodbye, Miles.

HUDDY MAKING PLANE
PLANE MADE

watch take off

WAVE AT AIRLINER

Sadness   Sad Huddy.